Marsh Pony

Fran Evans

Cai loved the marsh.

He loved the ponies that grazed the salty grasses.

He loved the pools filled with sea creatures . . .
and he loved the driftwood washed up by the tide.

At home, Cai shaped the driftwood into birds and boats
and beasts. Often he used shells and other seashore
treasures to decorate his models.

Sometimes he didn't know what he'd made
until it was finished.

At school, Cai sometimes brought in
his marsh creatures to show everyone.
'Fascinating,' said Mrs Williams.
'I like the crab,' said Siân.

But Jac and Joe were jealous.

'Stinky old rubbish,' they
jeered. 'Stinky old Cai.'

Down on the marsh, amongst the ponies, Cai could forget about the bullies.

He loved it when his friend, Celtie, splashed along the shore to greet him.

'Hello, boy,' said Cai happily.

Celtie followed Cai everywhere.

One day Cai was collecting wood for a special boat.
Suddenly Celtie snorted, ears pricked. He could
hear voices.

'Hey, bogtrotter!' called Jac.

'Scavenging on the shore again?' sneered Joe, kicking over Cai's treasures.

The boys laughed and ran off towards the old lighthouse.

Celtie nuzzled Cai's hair as he
gathered up his things.

A squally breeze startled the
herd. The tide was coming in . . .

Water gushed noisily up the
gullies, but Cai could hear
a different sound.

'Help! Help!'
 Jac and Joe were trapped.
'We can't swim!' they shouted,
clinging like limpets to the
lighthouse rocks.

Cai looked around . . . there was no one else to help.

'Come on, boy!' He urged Celtie into the surging tide.

'Hurry, Cai. Hurry!' whimpered the boys.
The water crept higher and higher and
higher . . .

'Climb onto Celtie's back!'
yelled Cai. 'What are you waiting for?
Quick! Jump! NOW!'

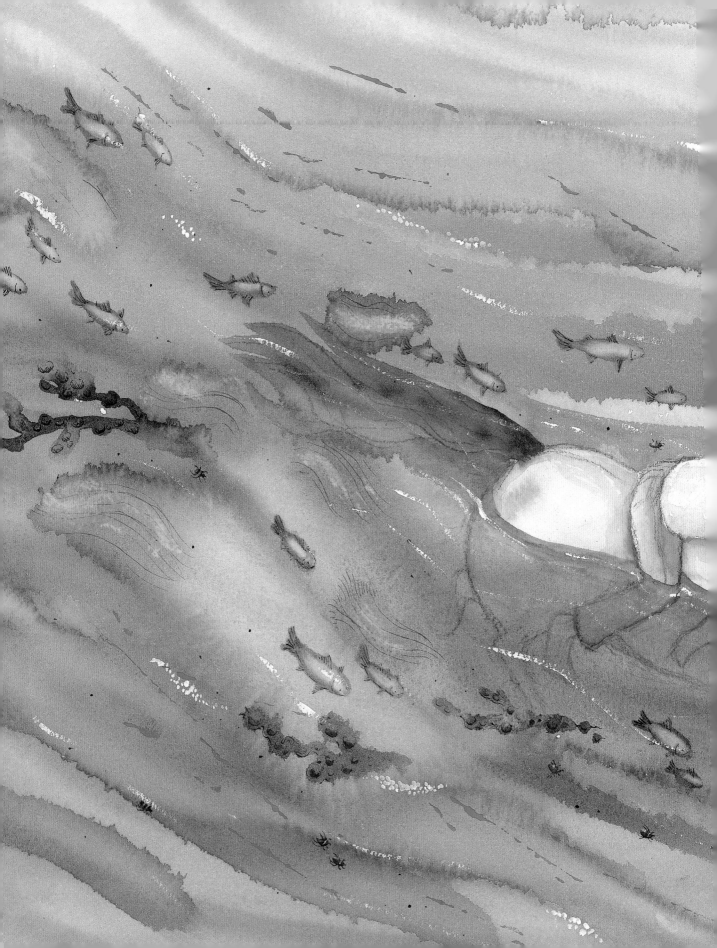

Jac and Joe thought their
nightmare would never end . . .

'I'm slipping,' panicked Joe, but Celtie dug
his hooves firmly into the marsh mud.

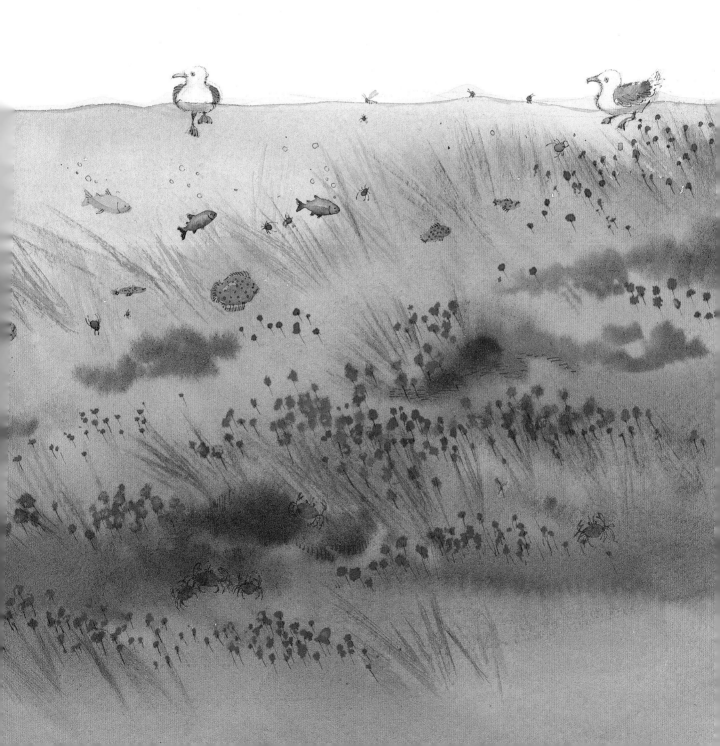

As Celtie reached dry land, the boys
tumbled into the shallows.

'Come on,' panted Cai. 'The tide's coming in fast.'

Once they were safe at Cai's house, Celtie
trotted away, whinnying to the herd.
'Bye, Celtie. Thanks for saving us!'
called the boys.

Cai grinned. 'You'd better
come in to get dry.'

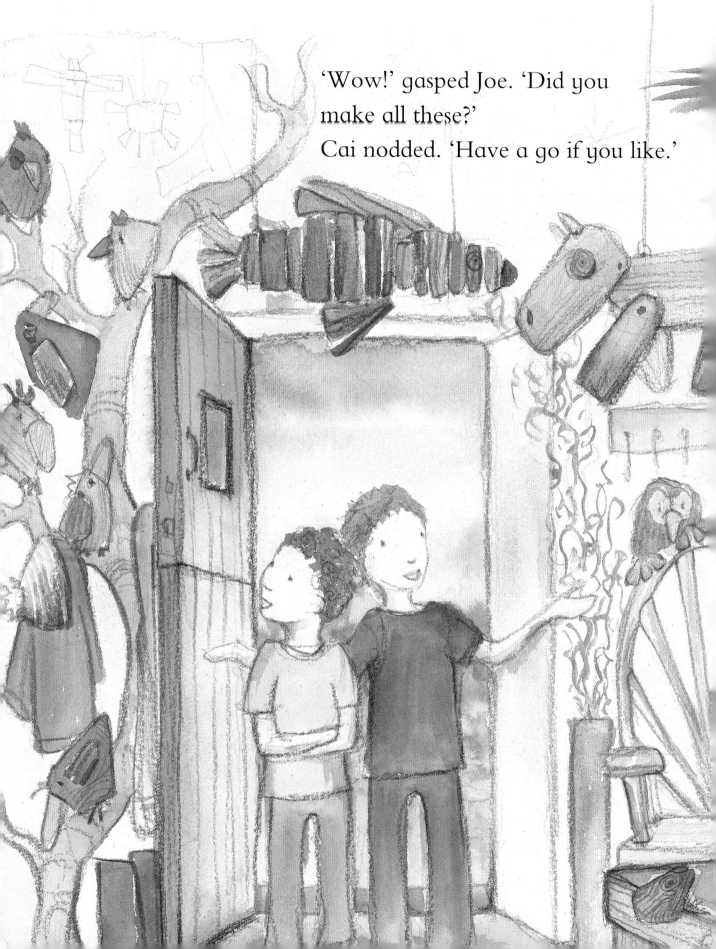

'Wow!' gasped Joe. 'Did you make all these?'
Cai nodded. 'Have a go if you like.'

He emptied his basket on the table.
'Cool!' said Joe. 'Can we really?'
Soon the boys were working happily together.

'See you tomorrow, Cai,' said
Joe when it was time to go.
    'Yeah, see you in school . . .'
said Jac. 'Thanks, Cai. We'll
always be friends now, won't
we, the three of us?'

'Don't forget Celtie!'
laughed Cai.

'Celtie for ever!' smiled Jac and Joe.

For Mike

First published in 2013 by Pont Books, an imprint of Gomer Press, Llandysul, Ceredigion, SA44 4JL

ISBN 978 1 84851 649 6

A CIP record for this title is available from the British Library.

This book is published with the financial support of the Welsh Books Council.

Printed and bound in Wales at Gomer Press, Llandysul, Ceredigion